Shira Shaked

Mr. Body and Mr. Feeling

Illustrations: Neta Grozki

Based on the **FSTR – Five Steps to Relief** method

developed by Shira Shaked

Producer & International Distributor
eBookPro Publishing
www.ebook-pro.com

Mr. Body and Mr. Feeling
Shira Shaked

Translation: Mathew Berman
Contact: shiraisthe1@gmail.com

To those who helped me along on this wonderful journey:

The Creator – For great is your loving kindness towards me (Psalms 86:13).

My children, who are so very dear to me

My beloved family

I love you.

Dear Parents, uncles and aunts, grandparents, therapists, and educators: Thank you for purchasing this book.

Hello, my name is Shira Shaked, nice to meet you. Over the years of my work as an Art Therapist, I have amassed a wealth of experience and knowledge. Over time, I began incorporating techniques that I learned in the world of body and feeling into my Art Therapy sessions. In using this mix of techniques, and using my own tools, I understood that I had created a method that gives people significant tools for emotional management. With the help of my method, people experience what it is to be empowered, and the tools provide considerable help managing an emotional process. That is how I created the **FSTR – Five Steps to Relief method.**

For the past few years, I have been instructing parents, children, educational teams and other therapists in the method, in order to pass on my knowledge. In my experience, the method is appropriate for all ages – adults as well as children. My goal is to expose as many people as possible to these tools and to help the public – this is what drove me to write this children's book. In the book, I brought together, in a way that is tailored to children, an empowering story based on the method for emotional balance that I have developed.

At the end of the book, you will find a practice sheet for using the method.

You and your children are welcome to write on it after you have read the book.

The content of the book deals with physical expressions of emotional reactions, and not physical ailments or illnesses. If a child has an emotional reaction to something, and after calming down continues to complain about any pain, please consider seeking medical counsel.

In case you want to delve deeper into the subject of emotional balance and acquire these skills, I teach a course on the FSTR method online. You can sign up for it and receive tools for life. Please feel free to contact me.

Similarly, there are Mr. Body and Mr. Feeling dolls, available for purchase.

Pleasant reading,

Shira

Hello kids, let's meet Johnny.
Johnny is a 6-year-old boy who is
in the first grade.
He is a smart, curious, creative,
and talented boy,
just like you, dear children,
who are reading and listening to
this story right now.

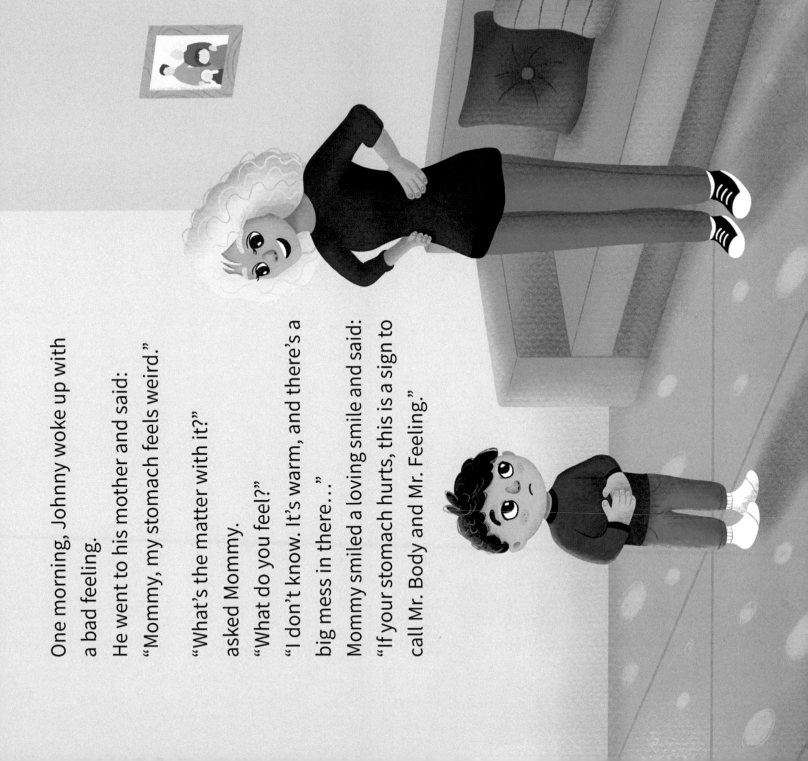

One morning, Johnny woke up with
a bad feeling.
He went to his mother and said:
"Mommy, my stomach feels weird."

"What's the matter with it?"
asked Mommy.
"What do you feel?"
"I don't know. It's warm, and there's a
big mess in there…"
Mommy smiled a loving smile and said:
"If your stomach hurts, this is a sign to
call Mr. Body and Mr. Feeling."

"Who are they?" Johnny asked, surprised.

"In order to meet them, let's use our imagination together, just as if you were dreaming a dream, or imagining that you're a superhero that can do anything."

"I know what imagining is! That's when I'm inside my own thoughts, sailing a boat at sea and making up new things!"

"That's right," Mommy said.

"And this time, concentrate on your aching stomach, and you can listen to Mr. Body and Mr. Feeling. They both exist inside of you, and they talk to you. Sometimes we hear them, and sometimes we don't, and if we ignore them, they start to really shout at us, to get us to listen to them."

"But what do they have to do with what's going on inside my stomach, Mommy? It hurts, and I don't like it at all."

"Let's listen to what Mr. Body and Mr. Feeling have to say," said Mommy, "And together we'll figure out what's going on in your stomach."

"Ok," said Johnny, curious to meet both of them, neither of whom he had ever heard of before.

Johnny closed his eyes. "I wonder what they look like" ... Johnny thought.

And then, when he entered the world of his imagination, they suddenly appeared in front of him.

"Hello, I'm Mr. Body. Nice to meet you. I'm responsible for telling you the things your body wants to say to you. Basically, I'm the voice of your body!"

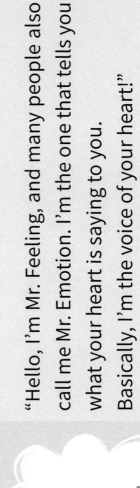

"Hello, I'm Mr. Feeling, and many people also call me Mr. Emotion. I'm the one that tells you what your heart is saying to you. Basically, I'm the voice of your heart!"

"I see them!" said Johnny to Mommy, his eyes still closed. "They're here with me!"

"Great!" said Mommy, "and I'm here with you."

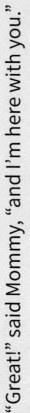

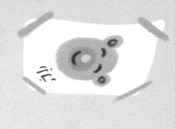

"Did you guys know that I woke up today with a terrible stomachache? Like, all messed up…"

"Where's this mess at?" asked Mr. Body.

"It's in my stomach and it really bothers me. It hurts, and it's warm," answered Johnny.

"Let's get in touch with your body and imagine what it's like in there."

"What does the mess look like? What color is it?" asked Mr. Body.

"It looks like a really big black and red whirlpool," said Johnny.

"And it's completely messed up," he emphasized.

"And where else is this mess in your body?
In your hands? In your legs? In your head?"
Johnny took a breath and, in his imagination,
scanned other parts of his body,
in order to see if they were also messed up.

"No, only in my stomach," he said afterwards.
"But in my whooole stomach…"
He placed his hand on his aching belly.

Mr. Feeling joined them and asked:
"Johnny, did you know that Mr. Body, my twin, tells me
when he feels things in the body, because we are connected?
We were born together and we're connected: Body and feeling,
body and heart, body and spirit.
Conne-c-ted!"

"But sometimes, people get confused and separate us,"
Mr. Body continued, "and that's sad.
That happens when they get really excited and confused,
And they forget that their emotions and their
bodies are connected!
If more people got to know us, they would reveal
all the secrets of the gifts they have inside
them and all their internal strength!"

"Inside each one of us is a special, important gift.

If we recognize it and use it,

we can discover an awesome power inside ourselves

that will help us!"

"What is this power?" Johnny asked.

"It's a natural ability we have, a power and strength that

is found inside of us," Mommy said.

"Wow, Mommy, how is it that I didn't know about this

power before?

How is it that I never knew about this gift inside me?"

Johnny asked in amazement.

"Come and I'll tell you, Johnny, because you're old

enough and mature enough to learn about it.

All the children listening now to this story are also old

enough and can learn about their gift that is inside them."

"So what do we do now?" asked Johnny.

"Now, we can communicate with Mr. Feeling since he and I are connected."

"Johnny, can you think why your tummy is bothering you?" asked Mr. Feeling.

"What bothers you so much and is causing you a problem?" they both asked together.

Johnny took another breath and said, "Yesterday, my sister was bothering me in my room. I wanted to say something, but kept quiet. At school during recess, a boy in my class took the ball that I brought to play with, and that really annoyed me! But he was very strong, so I just let it go and didn't say anything this time either," Johnny said with an angry face.

"Aha!" said Mr. Feeling. "Now I understand! You are feeling anger and frustration because of your sister and the boy from your class!

You let things go, you didn't say anything, and you didn't pay any attention to your feelings.

They stayed in your stomach, and now it really bothers you. Is that what you're feeling?"

"Yes," said Johnny, "that's exactly what I'm feeling, and I am really angry!

How can I feel better?" he asked.

"Don't worry, we're here to help you," they both said.

"The first thing we understood is that the pain is only in your stomach,

and now we know that the anger you experience is only one part of you,

and you have many other parts in you, like curiosity, creativity, friendship, and love."

"The pain in your body is a feeling that comes from the heart. And since we are paying attention to it now,

We can show it our appreciation by saying 'thank you.'"

"That helped me calm down, thanks! I already feel better!" said Johnny.

"Great! That's fantastic," said Mr. Feeling.

"And who decides what you do with your body, Johnny? Who's in charge of your body?"

"I am!" said Johnny, "Only I decide for myself!"

"That's right!" said Mr. Body.
"You are the only one who can decide for your body,
to choose what to do and how to behave!
So let's choose an activity together,
we will breathe slowly, and that way
we will calm your stomach down."

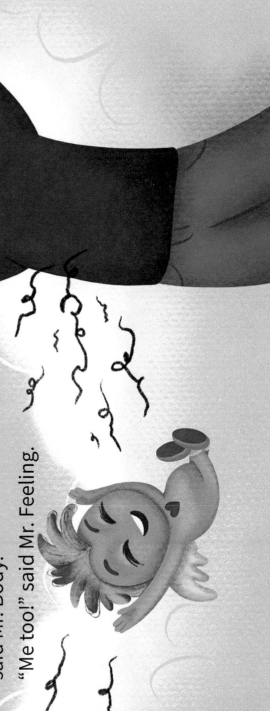

"And now that your stomach is more relaxed, you can talk
to the people that made you angry.

If you share with them how you feel,

you won't need to hold all that emotion and hurt inside,

and your problems with them can be solved!"

"That's right!" said Johnny, "there are a lot of things

that I can do!

In my body, I have gifts and the power

to help myself feel good!"

"I can do it!

I have strength and power!

My stomach already feels much better.

As if the whoole mess has gone away!"

"I'm so happy to hear that!"

said Mr. Body.

"Me too!" said Mr. Feeling.

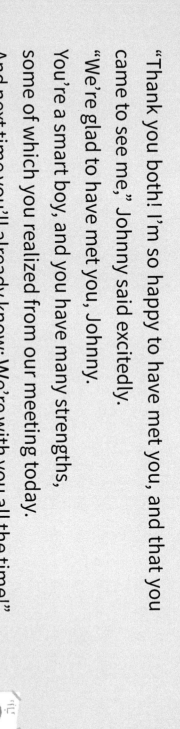

"Thank you both! I'm so happy to have met you, and that you came to see me," Johnny said excitedly.

"We're glad to have met you, Johnny.
You're a smart boy, and you have many strengths, some of which you realized from our meeting today.
And next time you'll already know: We're with you all the time!"

"Thank you, Mom, for calling Mr. Body and Mr. Feeling.
Now I know that each time I pay attention to my body and listen to what the feeling in my heart tells me, I will be reminded of this meeting with you guys.
I will smile to myself and know that you are always with me."

"Good for you, Johnny, that's wonderful!" said Mr. Body and Mr. Feeling.

"Thank you, Mom, for inviting us."

And now, we turn to you, dear children, in order to teach you about the wonderful gifts that you have inside you.

Worksheet - The FSTR method, Five Steps to Relief:

With this worksheet, you can practice with children, an incident in which they coped with feelings and sensations in the body, after an event/occurrence.

The first line shows a description of what we are doing, and the second line gives an example of how to practice using the method.

You are welcome to write and draw on the page.

Happy practicing! ☺

In the event that you want to dive deeper into the subject, and learn more, you can contact me to sign up for the full course of the FSTR method.

Similarly, Mr. Body and Mr. Feeling dolls are also available for sale.

For more on Shira and the FSTR method, you can contact by:

Email: shiraisthe1@gmail.com

Website:

FSTR method
Five Steps To Relief

Step1	Step 2	Step 3	Step 4	Step 5	End, and resolution
Connect to our body and identify the feeling/emotion	**Draw the location, size, shape, color, image of the feeling/emotion in the body**	**Scan the body and area where the feeling comes from and define where it is and isn't**	**Find the emotional reaction to the sensation/feeling in the body**	**Choose a helpful activity**	**Act to resolve the situation after understanding the connection between the body and the emotion**
Mess/hurt	Stomach, big red circle	Only in the stomach – not in the head, arms or legs	Anger at kids who bothered me	I choose to calm down by washing my face	Talk to the kid who bothered me, go tell the teacher, talk to my parents

Made in United States
Orlando, FL
17 April 2023

3220847 9R00018